To Helen, with many thanks for the inspiration.
And to my dad, who always did my hair just right. A.B.

To Jenny and Rosemary, for teaching me to dance. T.M.

With thanks to Miss Gregory and Miss Webb
at the Jill Stew School of Dance for inviting us to watch
Abbie, Grace, Holly, Madeleine and Nell's ballet class,
helping to inspire the illustrations for this book.

OXFORD
UNIVERSITY PRESS

Great Clarendon Street, Oxford OX2 6DP
Oxford University Press is a department of the University of Oxford.
It furthers the University's objective of excellence in research, scholarship,
and education by publishing worldwide in

Oxford   New York

Auckland Cape Town Dar es Salaam Hong Kong Karachi
Kuala Lumpur Madrid Melbourne Mexico City Nairobi
New Delhi Shanghai Taipei Toronto

With offices in

Argentina Austria Brazil Chile Czech Republic France Greece
Guatemala Hungary Italy Japan Poland Portugal Singapore
South Korea Switzerland Thailand Turkey Ukraine Vietnam

Oxford is a registered trade mark of Oxford University Press
in the UK and in certain other countries

Text copyright © Ann Bonwill 2011
Illustrations copyright © Teresa Murfin 2011

The moral rights of the illustrator have been asserted
Database right Oxford University Press (maker)

First published in 2011

British Library Cataloguing in Publication Data
Data available

ISBN: 978-0-19-272851-7 (hardback)
ISBN: 978-0-19-272852-4 (paperback)
1 3 5 7 9 10 8 6 4 2

Printed in China

Paper used in the production of this book is a natural,
recyclable product made from wood grown in sustainable forests.
The manufacturing process conforms to the environmental
regulations of the country of origin.

Naughty Toes

 Ann Bonwill ★ TERESA MURFIN

OXFORD
UNIVERSITY PRESS

My sister, Belinda, is a ballerina.
I, Trixie, am not.

When we go to Davida's Dance Shoppe
to pick out our leotards, shoes, and socks,
Belinda picks classic pink and white.

I pick red and purple and green.
'Are you sure?' asks Mum.

'I'm sure,' I say.
'It has style,' I say.

But the next day in class I'm not so sure.

Madame Mina
walks round the
room and looks
at our feet.

'Point!'
she says.

'Turn out!'
she says.

'Good toes,'
she says to Belinda.

'Naughty toes,'
she says to me.

Madame Mina claps the beat
while Mr Tiempo plays the music
on his sunny yellow piano.
'One, two, three, one, two, three.'

Somehow, I'm always on four.
'Naughty toes!' I hear above the notes of the piano.

Before our next class, Dad does our
hair in front of the mirror. He brushes
Belinda's hair straight back
into a bun, all neat and tidy.

She looks like a swan.

Mine sticks out all over like dandelion
fuzz. Dad sighs a long sigh as he tries
to tuck in the ends.

'Never mind,' I say.
'It's unique,' I say.

In class we do expressive dance.
'*Sway* like flowers!' says Madame Mina.
'*Flutter* like butterflies!'

It's hard to be a flower
when you need to go to the toilet.

'*Float* like clouds!'
says Madame Mina,

and I **spin** round the
room like a dust cloud,

clap like a thunder cloud,

whoosh like
a rain cloud . . .

SMACK!
straight into Bertram.

'What were you thinking?' asks Madame Mina.
'I was a cloud with gusto,' I say. Before I hang my
head, I think I see Mr Tiempo smiling.

'Your palms are spotlights,' says Madame Mina, 'shining brightly on your face.' I wave mine around so they'll sparkle on me like a disco ball.

'Trixie!' says Madame Mina in a very loud voice.
'It's jazzy,' I say in a very quiet voice.
Mr Tiempo is definitely smiling now.

After class Mum takes us out
for ice cream. Belinda orders plain
vanilla and eats it without drips.

I order pink-bubble-gum-swirl and try to
eat it very carefully . . . but somehow it spills.
Maybe I should have picked the pink leotard after all.

When it's time for the show, Belinda is the fairy princess. She wears a blue sequinned tutu and turns twirls on the stage.

I am a rock!

I am all in grey and stand still on the stage. It is hard to show spirit when you are a rock.

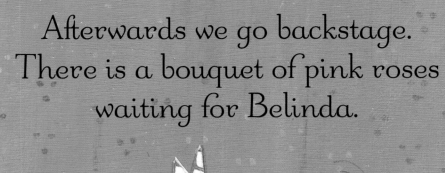

Afterwards we go backstage.
There is a bouquet of pink roses
waiting for Belinda.

It has a note that says,
'For my prima ballerina,
with love from Madame Mina.'

For me there is a cardboard box
tied up with red string. It has a
note that says, 'Follow your feet.'
I peek inside . . .

My sister, Belinda, is a ballerina.
I, Trixie . . .

. . . am a tap dancer!